DUMB CHOCOLATE EYES

KEVIN BROOKS

First published in 2015 in Great Britain by
Barrington Stoke Ltd
18 Walker Street, Edinburgh, EH3 7LP

www.barringtonstoke.co.uk

This story first appeared in a different
form in *Thirteen* (Orchard Books, 2005)

Text © 2005 Kevin Brooks
Illustrations © 2015 Emma Shoard

The moral right of Kevin Brooks and Emma
Shoard to be identified as the author and
illustrator of this work has been asserted
in accordance with the Copyright, Designs
and Patents Act, 1988

A CIP catalogue record for this book is
available from the British Library upon
request

ISBN: 978-1-78112-451-2

Printed in China by Leo

CONTENTS

CHAPTER 1
ONE OF THOSE THINGS

I never really liked Pete Cassidy.

I spent a lot of time with him, and I suppose you could say we were friends. But I don't think we ever meant that much to each other. It was a friendship based on convenience more than anything else. We lived in the same village, we went to the same school, we both turned 15 at the start of last summer ...

But that was about as far as it went.

I mean, we did stuff together, and sometimes we talked about things, but there was never anything more to it than that. In fact, when I look back on it now, I don't think we ever really *knew* each other at all. It was just one of those things, you know?

Pete would say to me, "You wanna come round my place?"

And I'd say, "Yeah ..."

It wasn't supposed to mean anything.

CHAPTER 2
A PERFECT MIXTURE

It's hard to describe Cassidy as anything more than average. He was average height, average size, with an average-looking face. His eyes were a bit on the weird side – kind of loose and lazy and chocolate brown. But apart from that, there wasn't anything out of the ordinary about him.

His home, on the other hand, was out of this world.

It was a bungalow, for one thing. I could never understand that. I mean, what's the point of a house with only one floor? What's *that* all about? And, for another thing, all the rooms were low and dark, and they were all connected, like a maze of tunnels ... and there were *loads* of them. It was ridiculous. It must have been like living in a rabbit warren.

Whenever I went there, I could never work out where anything was. In fact, I got lost once or twice ... coming back from the bathroom usually. That was kind of embarrassing.

"Just off to the toilet," I'd say. "Back in a minute."

Only I wouldn't be back in a minute, I'd be back in about half an hour. And then Cassidy would give me a funny look. Like, 'What the hell have you been doing?' And I wouldn't know what to say, so I'd just grin like a fool and pretend that everything was OK.

I don't suppose it would have mattered so much if we'd been better friends. I would have just told him that I'd got lost. Then he would have laughed and called me an idiot, and I would have said it was his fault for having such a stupid house ... and everything would have been OK.

The good thing was, whenever I went round to Cassidy's place we spent most of our time in the garden, so I didn't have to worry too much about getting lost in his house. All I had to worry about was getting lost in his garden.

His garden was *huge*.

I mean, the first time I saw it, I couldn't believe it. Up until then, the only gardens I'd ever seen were all pretty much the same. They all had a patch of lawn at the back of the house, a few flower beds, maybe a couple of bushes. But Cassidy's garden was something else.

Cassidy's garden was a rambling wilderness that seemed to go on for ever. It had acres of land, dozens of sheds and outbuildings, fields of wild grass and weeds, trees, broken walls, bits of old statues, ponds, greenhouses ... there was even an empty swimming pool, hidden away at the bottom of the garden. It was all cracked and flaky and dead-eyed blue.

KEVIN BROOKS

It was that kind of place.

A perfect mixture of paradise and hell.

CHAPTER 3
ONLY A RAT

Anyway, on the day I want to tell you about, me and Cassidy were hunting for rats in his garden.

It was Cassidy's idea. He'd seen this rat the day before. It was scuttling around by the empty swimming pool, and Cassidy thought it'd be a good idea to catch it and kill it. I couldn't see the point myself. It was only a rat ... why not just leave it alone? It wasn't doing any harm, was it?

"It's a *rat*," Cassidy sneered. "You don't leave rats alone."

"Why not?" I said.

"Because they're *rats*, that's why," he sneered. "They're pests, they carry diseases ..."

"What kind of diseases?" I asked.

"I dunno ..." he said. "Rat diseases."

"I've never heard of anyone catching a disease from a rat," I said.

"Yeah, well ... what do *you* know?"

I didn't know how to answer that, so I just shrugged.

"Anyway," Cassidy went on. "This isn't just any old rat – it's a monster. I mean, it's *really* big – big as a cat."

"Maybe it *is* a cat?" I said.

Cassidy rolled his eyes. "I think I know the difference between a cat and a rat."

"Yeah?"

Cassidy looked at me then, and there was something in his eyes that told me I'd better shut up. This was his house, his garden, and if I didn't like the idea of killing a rat ... well, I could always go home,

couldn't I?

And that was the funny thing, I suppose. I *could* have gone home. I could have said, "OK, Pete, I think I'll be going now. I'll see you later – all right?" And it *would* have been all right. He wouldn't have cared. I wouldn't have cared. It wouldn't have meant anything to either of us.

So why did I stay?

I don't know.

CHAPTER 4
JUNK

So, no, I didn't go home that day.

I suppose it was just another one of those things.

You know how it is.

You're at someone else's place, and they're doing something you're not quite sure about. You know in your heart that you'd rather not be there, but you just can't bring yourself to do anything about it …

Anyway, I didn't say anything else to Cassidy about the rat. I just lowered my eyes and looked at the ground and waited for the moment to pass. And, after a while, it did. I heard him sniff a couple of times. Then, when I looked up, he grinned at me and carried on talking as if nothing had happened.

"Yeah," he said, "and the thing is, when you see one rat, you always know there's going to be more. They breed like rabbits. I bet there's *hundreds* of them around here …"

'Breed like rabbits?' I thought. 'First they're as big as cats, and now they breed like rabbits? What kind of rats are we dealing with here?'

But I kept my thoughts to myself. I just nodded, like I knew what Cassidy was talking about. Then I followed him around the back of the bungalow and down into the

cellar of one of the outbuildings.

DUMB CHOCOLATE EYES

I could never understand why his house and the outbuildings had so many basements and cellars. They didn't seem to serve any purpose. As far as I could tell, Cassidy's family used them to hide away piles of rubbish – sacks of rotten seeds, bags of solid cement, coils of rusty wire, chairs with legs missing, old bike frames ... you know the kind of thing.

It seemed a bit odd to me that anyone would keep tons of useless old junk under their house. I almost asked Cassidy about it once. "Hey," I was going to say, "how come you've got so many cellars full of rubbish?" But I chickened out at the last minute. I was scared of how he might react.

"You *what?*" I imagined him saying. "What kind of stupid question is *that*? What's it got to do with you, anyway?"

Or maybe he'd just say, "Uh?"

That was the thing with Cassidy – you could never quite tell how he'd react to anything. Sometimes you'd get a laugh, sometimes a grunt, and other times you'd just get a look from those mad brown eyes.

I guess that's why I never asked him very much. It wasn't that I was *scared* to

ask him things, it was more a case of …
well, why risk a dirty look for the sake of
some useless information? I mean, who
cares what a cellar is for, anyway? It's a
cellar, that's all. It's just a cellar.

And that's that.

CHAPTER 5
UNDERGROUND

So, anyway, there we were in this dusty old cellar. Cassidy was searching around for rat traps, and I was sitting on a pile of old newspapers while I watched him.

I have to admit it felt pretty nice down there. Kind of cool and quiet, with that weird sort of underground feeling to the air. It was the kind of feeling that makes

you think that the rest of the world doesn't
exist.

Cassidy's face was a picture of dim-witted desire as he rummaged around in the underground junk.

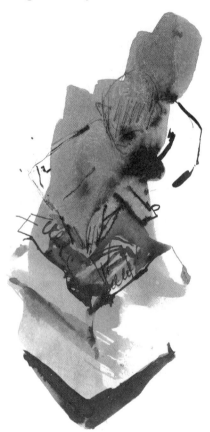

His eyes were narrowed, his brow was furrowed, his nose was twitching. He looked a bit like a determined animal searching for something to eat.

"Where are you?" he kept mumbling to himself. "Come on, where are you? I know you're in here somewhere …"

The more he searched, the dustier the air became. He dug around, flung things to one side, and after a while the whole cellar was clouded with a browny-grey haze.

I could taste the dust in the back of my throat, and I could feel it clogging up my nose. It smelled quite nice, believe it or not – kind of old and earthy and warm. In fact, there was something quite nice about the whole thing. As I sat there, breathing in the dust and the underground air, it would have been easy for me to have closed my eyes and nodded off for a while.

But then I heard a harsh clatter of metal and a sudden cry. "Gotcha!"

And my moment of peace was broken.

I looked up through the dust and saw that Cassidy was burrowing down into a cardboard box. He grabbed at something with both hands, and then he stood up and turned to me. He had a grin of triumph on his face and a rusty old rat trap dangling from each hand.

"Look at these!" he said. He waved the traps at me. "What d'you think? You ever seen anything like this before? Look at the *size* of 'em!"

"Yeah," I agreed, "they're pretty big."

And they were. Imagine a mouse trap – the old-fashioned kind that snaps down and chops off the mouse's head. Then imagine how it'd look if it was four times bigger … well, that's what Cassidy was holding in his hands. They were nasty, evil, ugly things.

"There's loads of them, look," Cassidy said. He bent down to the cardboard box again. "I reckon there's about a dozen in here."

There was a dark fire in his eyes as he lifted up the box.

"Come on, let's get out of here," he said. "You take the traps down to the pool and I'll go and get some bread." He looked at me. I hadn't moved. "Here," he said, and he passed me the box. "Come *on*. What's the matter with you? You wanna catch rats or not?"

I stood up and followed Cassidy out of the cellar.

CHAPTER 6
EMPTY

I'm not sure what I thought about while I stood by the empty pool and waited for Cassidy to come back with the bread.

I might have wondered what I was doing there, standing beside an empty swimming pool with a cardboard box full of rat traps at my feet. But I probably didn't. I probably just stood there and looked around, not thinking about anything. Just looking around and waiting for Cassidy to come back ...

I really can't remember. It was just another moment, you know? Another moment, another day, another bit of life.

It didn't mean anything.

Why should it?

At last I saw Cassidy coming back. He was half running across the garden and he had a bag of sliced white bread in his hand.

"This should do it," he said, and he waggled the bread at me.

"Do rats like bread?" I asked him. "I thought they liked cheese."

"That's mice," he said. "Rats eat anything. They're hombivores."

"Omnivores," I corrected him.

"What?"

"Omnivores," I said again. "Animals that eat anything are called omnivores."

"I know – that's what I *said*." He shook his head at me, like I was an idiot, then he opened the bag of bread and pulled out a slice.

I watched him as he crouched down and took one of the rat traps out of the box.

"You've got to watch your fingers," he told me, as he set the trap with bread. "A friend of my dad's lost a thumb when he was setting up one of these."

I raised my hand and wiggled my fingers in front of my face.

I tried to imagine myself without a thumb. It made me feel kind of shivery.

"Right," Cassidy said. "That's the first one done. Eleven more to go."

I didn't set any traps myself. I just followed Cassidy around the garden. I carried the box, passed him the traps, prepared the bread, listened to what he had to say. I think he saw himself as the master rat-catcher ... and me as his apprentice.

"The thing is," he told me, "you don't want to put the traps too close together. Rats aren't stupid. If one of them gets caught and the others see him lying there dead, they'll get worried. D'you see what I mean? They'll start to think that something's going on ..."

"They'll smell a rat," I joked.

"Yeah," Cassidy said, not getting it. "Rats can smell things from miles away. They can see in the dark, too. I told you, they're not stupid."

He made it sound like a reason for killing them.

"How much bread have we got left?" he asked me.

I looked in the bag. "Half a slice."

"Give it here."

I passed him the last piece of bread. He bit off half of it, chewed it for a while, then spat it out into his hand and rolled it into a ball.

"D'you want this?" he said. He offered me the bit of the bread he hadn't chewed.

"Uh ... no, thanks," I told him.

"You sure? There's nothing wrong with it."

I smiled and shook my head.

"Suit yourself." He shrugged and popped the bread into his mouth as he carried on with the final trap. "No point in wasting it."

CHAPTER 7
THE KITCHEN

When all the rat traps were set and laid out around the garden, we went inside to wait.

It's hard to remember exactly what we did while we were waiting. I remember following Cassidy along the maze of tunnels to his room, so I guess we spent some time in there, but I don't know what we did. Not much, I guess. I expect we just did what we usually did – hang around, look at stuff, maybe play a couple of Xbox games. Cassidy had one of those football games – not the action kind, but the kind where you're the manager. You have to pick your players and do all the transfers and stuff. Sometimes he played it when I was there, which was pretty boring for me. All he would do was sit in front of the screen for hours, searching through lists of players.

"What are you doing?" I'd ask him.

"Uh?"

"What are you doing?"

He'd say something like, "I'm trying to buy a right-footed centre-back for less than ten million quid."

"Oh," I'd say.

And that would be that.

So, maybe that's what we did while we waited in his room. Maybe I sat there and pretended to read a magazine while Cassidy tried to buy a right-centred back foot for less than ten zillion quid ... or maybe not. Like I said, I just can't remember.

But I'm pretty sure that after a while we went into the kitchen for biscuits and juice.

We must have, because that's what we always did.

And, also, I remember seeing Cassidy's mum that day, and the only place I ever saw her was in the kitchen.

She was a funny little woman, Mrs Cassidy. She was kind of small and timid, and she never said anything. Even when she was dishing out the biscuits and juice, she never said a word. She just scuttled around with a nervous smile on her face. She seemed to spend a lot of her time doing that.

Cassidy's dad was a scuttler, too. He was always dressed in blue overalls, and he always looked busy, but I never saw him actually doing anything. Cassidy had an older brother, too – an ugly thing called

Wayne. I can't think of much to say about him. He had a fat belly and a fat head, and he thought he was smart, but he wasn't.

But at least he didn't scuttle.

CHAPTER 8
PAUSE IN THE AIR

We must have spent about an hour in the kitchen, and then me and Cassidy went back outside to check on the traps. I still had the taste of cheap biscuits and watery orange juice in my mouth, and I was kind of desperate to use the toilet. But Cassidy was in a hurry.

"C'mon, c'mon, let's go ..." he jabbered.

And then I thought that if I *did* go to the bathroom I'd probably only get lost again. So I just gritted my teeth and followed Cassidy as he scuttled out into the garden. He couldn't wait to get to the traps. He was all flappy and over-excited, like a kid on Christmas morning, and his eyes were blinking and twitching like mad. It was a bit scary, to be honest. I was beginning to think there was something a bit psycho about him.

"How many rats d'you reckon we've got?" he said. "Four? Six? Ten? What d'you think?"

I got the feeling he was talking to himself, so I didn't bother answering.

I could see most of the traps now. I could see Cassidy ahead of me as he hurried over to the nearest one.

"OK," he said, all out of breath. "Here we go, here we go ... let's see what we've got."

I saw him stop by the rat trap and look down at it, and I felt a kind of pause in the air. And then I was walking up beside him and looking down at what we'd done ... I don't think I'll ever forget it. Lying at our feet, its neck almost severed by the powerful trap, was a sparrow. One of its wings was sticking up into the air, and its beak was wide open in a silent scream.

"Christ," Cassidy said, and he looked around at the other traps.

And then he started laughing.

Every trap had a dead sparrow in its

jaws. Twelve traps – twelve dead sparrows.

Their little brown beaks were pearled with

blood and their lifeless feathers ruffled in the breeze.

Something died in me then.

I can't really explain it.

I just felt so bad.

So guilty, so stupid, so childish.

But I think the thing I felt worst about was my ignorance. I'd known all along that we were trying to kill rats, but it wasn't until we'd killed twelve sparrows that I finally realised what we were actually *doing*.

I hated myself for that.

I hated what we'd done.

And I hated Cassidy and his dumb chocolate eyes.

He was still standing beside me, still pointing at the traps, still laughing and giggling and snorting like a madman.

I felt so sick.

I couldn't speak.

I turned around and walked away.

CHAPTER 9
TWIST OF FATE

That was the last I ever saw of Pete Cassidy – a boy standing on his lawn laughing at twelve dead sparrows.

A couple of weeks later he was racing his bike down a hill in the village when he lost control and crashed into the path of an oncoming lorry. No one was to blame. It was just one of those things – an accident, a tragedy, a twist of fate.

Whatever it was, Cassidy died instantly.

And I still don't know how I feel about that.

ABOUT KEVIN BROOKS

Kevin Brooks was born in Exeter and now lives in North Yorkshire with his wife Susan and a bunch of animals. Before he became a full-time author of hard-hitting, compelling teen fiction, Kevin did too many things to mention and lived in too many places to remember. He has been a rock star, worked in a zoo, a crematorium and a post office. Kevin's brilliant novels have won many awards, most notably the 2014 Carnegie Medal for *The Bunker Diary*.

'**Kevin Brooks just gets better and better**' *Sunday Telegraph*

'**A masterly writer**' *Mail on Sunday*

Praise for *Johnny Delgado: Private Detective*

'**The breathtaking pace of the end of the book brings it to an energetic conclusion, but it is the subtext of compassion, loyalty and justice which ultimately gives the book its resonance**' *Books for Keeps*

Praise for *The Bunker Diary*

'**An exceptional, brave book that pulls no punches and offers no comfortable ending**' *CILIP Carnegie Medal Judges*

Our books are tested
for children and young people by
children and young people.

Thanks to everyone who consulted on
a manuscript for their time and effort in
helping us to make our books better
for our readers.